CW00850635

Brian Brackbrick and the

Hazard of Harry Hatman

Book 1 of 6

ISBN-10: 197836699X

ISBN-13: 978-1978366992

HARRY HATMAN'S
HAT SHOP
FOR HAT LOVERS

For DYLAN, OLLIE and OWEN

These stories are inspired by
the fun and laughter that you
bring with you.
Thank you for reminding me
that I was a little boy once who
loved to read!

People!

Brian Brackbrick

George Bum

Harry Hatman

Fancy Nancy Sprinkle

Dr. Harley Letters

Mr. Sparker

Places!

The New Hat Shop

The Library

The Cake Shop

Things!

An Over-Sized Bowler Hat

A Woolly Hat

CHAPTER 1:

BEST FRIENDS

Brian Brackbrick was a ten-year-old boy who lived in an ordinary house in an ordinary town.

It was only a small town, but it had a long main street with lots of shops, a library, a swimming pool, and a police station. It was a quiet, pleasant place to live – most of the time.

Every so often, someone would appear with a crazy idea or a dangerous plan or a deadly scheme, and Brian Brackbrick would have to stop them.

The three most important things to know about Brian Brackbrick were:

1 Brian Brackbrick was very fond of wearing hats, and he would never leave his home without wearing one.

2 Even though Brian Brackbrick was only ten years old, he was the one-hundred and thirty-eighth cleverest person in the whole world.

3 Brian Brackbrick's best friend in the whole world was the nicest, most helpful and loyal friend anyone could ever want – his name was George Bum.

George Bum was not one of the cleverest people in the world, and he quite often needed Brian Brackbrick to explain things to him.

George Bum was, though, definitely one of the **nicest** people in the world, and everybody liked him. (Well, everybody except Charlie Chipchase, but he didn't really like anybody, and no-one cared what Charlie Chipchase thought anyway.)

George Bum lived two doors down from Brian Brackbrick's house, and they had been the best of friends for as long as they could remember. They always walked to school and back together.

Charlie Chipchase lived in a very big house at the end of their street, but he had never wanted to play with them, and never ever walked to school with them. (Charlie Chipchase was only the two-hundred and fifty-third cleverest person in the whole world, and Brian Brackbrick thought maybe that was why he didn't like them.

George Bum always tried to be nice to Charlie Chipchase, but it didn't seem to work.)

During the school holidays, like now, Brian Brackbrick and George Bum would spend most of their time together, and would often walk along the main street, where all the shops were.

At the end of the main street was Brian Brackbrick's favourite place in the whole world, the Library.

Today was a lovely sunny day, and Brian Brackbrick and George Bum were ready to leave for another day of adventure. They were stopped, however, as Brian Brackbrick was faced with a terrible emergency, the worst kind of emergency – a Hat Emergency!

CHAPTER 2:

BRIAN BRACKBRICK HAS A HAT EMERGENCY

Brian Brackbrick had a lot of hats. Any type of hat you can think of, Brian Brackbrick had one.

Every morning, before leaving the house, Brian Brackbrick would stand in front of his enormous hat collection and choose a hat to wear for the day. Sometimes the choice would depend on the weather, or what time of year it was, or sometimes for no reason at all.

Brian Brackbrick had berets and Panama hats and smart caps for school; bowler hats for special occasions; straw boaters and baseball caps for summer; and big woolly hats and deerstalkers for winter. There was even an enormous Sombrero hat for parties.

This morning, Brian Brackbrick had decided to wear his light-coloured Panama hat, but could not find it anywhere.

“This is dreadful, terrible, the most horrible, shocking thing ever!” Brian Brackbrick declared to Mr. Brackbrick and Mrs. Brackbrick.

“What is it, Brian?” asked Mr. Brackbrick as he calmly put down his newspaper.

“I cannot find my light-coloured Panama hat anywhere!” said Brian Brackbrick. “I have searched all over the house, and it is nowhere to be found! Someone in this room has hidden my light-coloured Panama hat!”

“Um, Brian – ” interrupted George Bum, who had noticed that Mr. Brackbrick was moving uncomfortably in his armchair, as if he had sat on something.

"Do not worry, George," said Brian Brackbrick, "I know that you would never hide one of my hats!" said Brian Brackbrick.

George Bum kept trying to interrupt. "No, I wouldn't do that, Brian, but, you see – "

"A-ha!" shouted Brian Brackbrick, as Mr. Brackbrick reached underneath him and pulled out a rather squashed light-coloured Panama hat. "The mystery is solved."

Mr. Brackbrick handed the squashed and sorry-looking hat to him. "I'm ever so sorry, Brian. I didn't see it there when I sat down."

Brian Brackbrick took the squashed hat from Mr. Brackbrick with a sad face.

Mr. Brackbrick knew how important hats were to Brian Brackbrick, and he knew what would cheer him up. “Looks like you need a new hat, Brian,” said Mr. Brackbrick, reaching into his pocket, and Brian Brackbrick burst into a huge smile straight away. "Here is some money."

Brian Brackbrick handed the note to George Bum straight away without even looking at it. (Brian Brackbrick was not concerned with money at all, and found the whole idea very strange indeed, thinking that everyone should simply have the things they needed. Luckily, George Bum was very good with money.)

"Go to the new hat shop in town," Mr. Brackbrick said, "and get yourself a new hat. This is your chance to see what the new hat shop owner is like."

"What do you mean?" said a shocked Brian Brackbrick. "Whatever happened to Old Mr. Hatston?"

Old Mr. Hatston ran the hat shop in town, called:

It was Brian Brackbrick's favourite shop in town.

"It seems that Old Mr. Hatston has retired," said Mr. Brackbrick. "It was rather sudden, now I think about it. Anyway, the hat shop looks rather different this morning. I think it's called 'Harry Hatman's Hat Shop for Hat Lovers' now."

"There is no time to lose, George," said Brian Brackbrick, as he grabbed a baseball cap and fixed it firmly on his head (as he would never leave the house without a hat). "Let us go and meet Harry Hatman!"

CHAPTER 3:

BARRY BACKSPLASH FALLS OVER

Brian Brackbrick and George Bum made their way through the town, along the main street where all the shops were, towards the hat shop.

The hat shop was in between the flower shop on one side, and the cake shop on the other. The cake shop was run by Nancy Sprinkle, and was called Fancy Nancy's Cakes, Puddings, Pies, Cakes, Pastries, Flans & Cakes.

Brian Brackbrick and George Bum had saved the cake shop from a terrible and very messy Yoghurt Inferno last summer, and could now get free cakes whenever they popped in.

The flower shop was run by Mrs. Broomhilda Blumenhole, and was called Precious Petals and Dazzling Displays of Brilliant Blooms for All Occasions.

Brian Brackbrick knew that Mrs. Blumenhole had been very good friends with Old Mr. Hatston, so she may know what had happened to him.

That was a question for another time, though. Brian Brackbrick needed a new hat right away!

The new hat shop was indeed called Harry Hatman's Hat Shop for Hat Lovers. When it had been Old Mr. Hatston's shop, it was quite dull to look at, mostly brown and beige, and quite dusty.

The new hat shop looked quite different – the outside of the shop was bright, shiny and colourful, and the sign gave the shop name in huge flashing lights.

Before they could go into the shop, the door opened and a man came stumbling out through the doorway. Brian Brackbrick and George Bum recognised him straight away – it was Barry Backsplash, who ran the town's swimming pool. (Brian Brackbrick was not a very good swimmer, but he always tried very hard; George Bum was a natural in the pool.)

Brian Brackbrick and George Bum were surprised to see Barry Backsplash wearing a swimming cap, as they knew that swimming caps were only for the swimming pool. (This is one reason why Brian Brackbrick liked swimming, despite not being very good at it – he liked any activity that you had to wear a hat for.) Barry Backsplash was also stumbling and tripping over his own feet, which was not like him at all.

Barry Backsplash finally tumbled over in front of the flower shop. Brian Brackbrick and George Bum bent down straight away to check if he was ok, and saw that the swimming cap had come loose and slipped from his head.

Barry Backsplash blinked as if he had just woken up, and looked at them both. “Hello lads,” said Barry Backsplash as he stood up, seemingly back to his normal self. “What’s all this then?”

“You fell over, Mr. Backsplash,” said Brian Brackbrick. “Do you feel okay?”

“Fell over? Me?” said Barry Backsplash. “Don’t be ridiculous, I would never fall over, or trip, or slip on a wet tile, or anything like that!”

This was rather puzzling, but Brian Brackbrick's thoughts were interrupted by a voice behind them. "Everything okay here, gentlemen?"

Everyone turned to see the town's police officer, Sergeant Shelley Shiplap.

"Absolutely fine, Sergeant Shiplap," said Barry Backsplash, "I don't know what all the fuss is about, no problems here."

"Well, I saw you fall over, Mr. Backsplash, are you sure you're alright?" asked Sergeant Shiplap.
"Fall over? Me?" said Barry Backsplash. "Don't be ridiculous, I would never –"

"Mr. Backsplash?" said George Bum. "You dropped your swimming cap."

Before Barry Backsplash could take it, Sergeant Shiplap snatched the swimming cap from George Bum's hand. "Interesting, a new cap, is it?"

"Well, yes, at least, I think so…" said Barry Backsplash, trying to remember.

"I think I'll just keep this as evidence for now," said Sergeant Shiplap. "I don't want people in my town falling over all over the place! Evening all!" she said – even though it was still morning – as she turned and strode away.

"I think I'd better get back to the swimming pool," said Barry Backsplash. "I'm not quite sure what I came out here to get."

Barry Backsplash walked away, looking puzzled, and Brian Brackbrick and George Bum finally opened the door of Harry Hatman's shop and walked in.

CHAPTER 4:
HARRY HATMAN

As Brian Brackbrick and George Bum walked into the shop, they almost had to shut their eyes against the glare.

It was very bright in there, and very clean, except for a few small leaves and petals scattered on the floor towards the back of the shop.

It was not at all like the dim and dusty shop of Old Mr. Hatston. Brian Brackbrick was surprised to see only a few hats on display.

The shelves were enormous, and very thick, and most had just one or two hats with a bright light above, shining right on them.

When it had been Old Mr. Hatston's shop, it might have been dark and dusty, but there had been hats everywhere.

Boxes and boxes of them, and big boxes filled with hatboxes, and even bigger boxes filled with those boxes.

Brian Brackbrick wondered what had happened to all those hats.

Just then Harry Hatman came out from the back of the shop, wearing bright yellow trousers and a bright yellow shirt, a bright red waistcoat and huge cowboy boots.

On his head, Harry Hatman was wearing the most enormous hat Brian Brackbrick and George Bum had ever seen (and they had seen a lot of hats).

Brian Brackbrick knew that it was called a Stetson or cowboy hat, and people would sometimes wear them in old cowboy films. They were supposed be big, but this was so big that it looked impossible for Harry Hatman to wear.

From the way he walked and the way he grinned at them, it seemed that Harry Hatman thought that he looked awesome.

He looked ridiculous.

Also, Harry Hatman seemed to have been waiting for Brian Brackbrick and George Bum.

"Hey there!" said Harry Hatman, only he made the "hey" last a very long time. It was more like this:

"H e e e e e e e e e e y y y y y y y y y there! Look who it is!" Harry Hatman rushed over to greet them, shaking their hands, and seemed very pleased indeed to meet them. "Why, if it isn't the legends of the town! You two are heroes around here! What brings you to my little hat shop today?"

Brian Brackbrick was lost for words, and this didn't happen very often. Ever since Harry Hatman had stepped out from the back of the shop, Brian Brackbrick's eyes had been fixed on the enormous, ridiculous Stetson hat.

It was George Bum who spoke first. "We're pleased to meet you, Mr. Hatman. I'm George Bum, and this is my best friend, Brian Brackbrick."

"Well I know who **you** are, boys!" said Harry Hatman. "I'm falling over with happiness that you have chosen to visit my hat shop."

"Do you know what happened to Old Mr. Hatston?" asked George Bum.

"Who? Never heard of him! Maybe **Mr. Sparker** didn't want him around anymore!" said Harry Hatman, adding, "oh, I've never heard of him either, no idea who that is! Anyway, I think I can guess why you're here! I think someone wants a new hat!"

The words 'new hat' snapped Brian Brackbrick out of it. "Yes, yes, that is it. I need a new hat, right away. A light-coloured Panama hat to replace one that was sadly squashed beyond repair."

"I've got just the thing!" shouted Harry Hatman as he reached behind the shop counter and brought up a hatbox. "A brand new, smart bowler hat!"

"I already have a bowler hat," said Brian Brackbrick. "It is a Panama hat that I need, Mr. Hatman."

"Ah!" said Harry Hatman. "You don't have one like this! It is an extra special, extra smart bowler hat! Why don't you try it on? Try it on right now!"

Brian Brackbrick looked at Harry Hatman as if he was talking nonsense. "That is ridiculous, crazy, the most absurd thing I have ever heard, Mr. Hatman! Today is simply not a bowler hat day!"

Harry Hatman looked puzzled, and almost annoyed for a moment, before he carried on. "Okay boys, I tell you what, you take this home and try it on first thing in the morning! I am certain that tomorrow will be a bowler hat day!"

Brian Brackbrick shrugged. “Well, I suppose that is possible.”

“That’s settled then! One extra smart bowler hat for young Mr. Brackbrick! No, no money is needed, you take it home and try it on first!”

Harry Hatman gave the hatbox to Brian Brackbrick and started to move them towards the door, just as it opened.

Stood in the doorway was Lord Mayor Spencer, the Mayor of the town. He was an impressive sight in his official Mayor’s hat, and Mayor’s robe, and heavy gold chains around his neck, and gold rings on his fingers, and his thick white beard.

His official title was Lord Mayor the Very and Right Honourable M'Lord the Lord Mayor (which is quite long, so let's go with Lord Mayor for short).

Lord Mayor Spencer looked and behaved as if he was very grand and important, but he didn't actually do very much in the town. It was Lord Mayor Spencer who would give out medals and awards when someone had done something very special or incredibly brave.

Brian Brackbrick and George Bum had been presented with lots of awards by Lord Mayor Spencer, most recently for saving Fancy Nancy's cake shop from the Yoghurt Inferno.

"HATMAN!" Lord Mayor Spencer shouted as he burst in, and then his voice changed when he saw Brian Brackbrick and George Bum. "Oh, hello you two! I didn't expect to see you here so soon, ho ho! I see you've met Mr. Hatman!

Didn't take you long to get to the new hat shop, eh? Ho ho."

Lord Mayor Spencer carried on before anyone else could speak. "Well, run along boys, I expect you've got other things to do, more things to stick your noses into, and all that! Ho ho. I must talk with Mr. Hatman at once! About my very special and very grand new Mayor's hat, which Mr. Hatman is making for me by hand! That's it, run along then!"

Lord Mayor Spencer ushered them out of the shop, carrying Brian Brackbrick's new hatbox, before they could say anything. It did seem a bit strange that Lord Mayor Spencer would need to talk to Harry Hatman so urgently. They were quickly distracted from these thoughts as they walked past Fancy Nancy's cake shop next door, and saw Nancy waving at them to come inside. This could mean only one thing: free cupcakes!

CHAPTER 5:

FREE CAKES FROM FANCY NANCY

Brian Brackbrick and George Bum pushed open the door of Fancy Nancy's cake shop and walked in.

Fancy Nancy's cake shop was so full of cakes and cakey things, it looked like it was made of icing, sponge and sweets. The display counter was full of every cake you could think of, all made by Nancy herself.

There were sponge cakes, chocolate cakes, fairy cakes, angel cakes, ginger cakes, rock cakes, coconut cakes, coffee cakes, walnut cakes, drizzle cakes, donuts, scones, pastries, cookies, meringues, fudge cakes, brownies, eclairs, iced buns, gateaux, Battenberg cakes, fruit cakes, fruit tarts, fruit flans, carrot cakes, cream cakes, and, of course, cupcakes.

Nancy could make any type of cake you could think of, out of whatever ingredients you wanted.

There was a table for people to sit at, shaped like a huge cake with white and green icing (some people said that this was actually a real cake, but no-one had ever tried to cut into it to find out), and comfy cushions on the floor shaped like giant white marshmallows.

"Hello boys, come on in!" said Nancy, walking over with a tray of cupcakes. Nancy liked to wear pink, and it was difficult to see where each piece of clothing began and ended. "Take a cupcake each, that's it! Always free for you two."

Brian Brackbrick and George Bum took a cupcake each from Nancy's tray and plopped down onto the marshmallow cushions.

"I'm glad you're here, boys, I've got something to show you." Nancy put her tray down on the counter and reached down behind it. She brought over a pile of folded t-shirts – pink, of course. "I'm thinking of selling other things as well as cakes – how about Fancy Nancy's very own line of t-shirts? Look at these."

Nancy unfolded each of the t-shirts and showed them to Brian Brackbrick and George Bum. Each one had a printed message on it, like –

– and things like that.

"What do you think?" Nancy asked them, with a hopeful smile.

Brian Brackbrick and George Bum didn't think Nancy would sell many of the t-shirts, but they didn't want to hurt Nancy's feelings.

"Well, they are very pink," said Brian Brackbrick. Which was true.

"They're very nice t-shirts, Nancy. I like them very much," said George Bum.

"Lovely, I knew you would like them," Nancy said, folding them back up again.

"Nancy?" asked Brian Brackbrick. "Do you know what happened to Old Mr. Hatston?"

"Would you like another cupcake, boys?" Nancy said, picking up her tray once again. "Have another cupcake!"

"No thank you, Nancy." Brian Brackbrick tried another question. "Have you met Harry Hatman yet? He is very different to Old Mr. Hatston."

"I have met him, yes," said Nancy, thoughtfully. "He's rather loud, and quite pushy. He's already brought three different hats over for me to try on. I don't even like hats."

Brian Brackbrick looked shocked to hear this.

"What I mean is," Nancy added, "I don't ever need to wear hats."

"Maybe he's trying to make friends, Nancy," said George Bum.

"Maybe," said Nancy. "I asked if he could get me some hair-nets – I always wear them when

I'm baking, so they would be useful – but he wasn't interested. On and on he went, asking me to try on his hats. He even brought over a bowler hat, can you imagine me wearing a bowler hat!"

Brian Brackbrick and George Bum both looked at the hatbox on the table…

"What about Old Mr. Hatston, Nancy? Where did he go?" asked Brian Brackbrick.

Nancy sighed. "I don't know, boys. He was there yesterday, in his dusty old shop. I saw him as I left – he was going into the flower shop to say good evening to Mrs. Blumenhole, as usual."

Nancy was silent for a moment.

"Then what happened, Nancy?" asked George Bum.

"Then I went home," said Nancy. "When I got here this morning, the hat shop had changed, and Harry Hatman was there. Very strange."

"Very strange indeed, Nancy," said Brian Brackbrick. "Harry Hatman mentioned someone called Mr. Sparker, do you know who that is?"

Nancy seemed to jump as if someone had startled her, and she dropped some of her cupcakes. George Bum got up straight away to help her pick them up.

"Whatever is the matter, Nancy?" asked Brian Brackbrick.

"Oh, nothing, nothing," said Nancy.

"So do you know Mr. Sparker, Nancy?" asked George Bum.

Nancy seemed to have gone quite pale. "No, I don't…well, yes, kind of…well, what I mean is, I've never met him. But I know who he is. He owns all of these shops – well, the buildings, anyway. We all have to pay rent to Mr. Sparker. It was the same when my dear mother ran this shop."

"But you have never met him?" asked Brian Brackbrick.

"No," said Nancy.

“So you don’t know what he looks like?” asked George Bum.

“No,” repeated Nancy.

“Interesting,” Brian Brackbrick said as he got up from the marshmallow cushion. “Let us go, George! There is one person who will know about all this!”

George Bum picked up the hatbox. “Do you mean – ”

“Yes, George!” said Brian Brackbrick. “To the library!”

CHAPTER 6:

THE MOST WONDERFUL PLACE IN TOWN

The library was right at the end of the main street where all the shops were. It was a big, grand old building, built of red brick and cream-coloured stone, and almost totally covered with climbing ivy, except for the roof and the windows.

The library was Brian Brackbrick's most favourite place in the whole world. The only thing that Brian Brackbrick liked as much as hats was books, and the library was crammed full of books, on any subject you could think of.

Brian Brackbrick would often go to the library and stay there for hours, reading book after book after book – he was the one-hundred and thirty-eighth cleverest person in the whole world, after all. (Sometimes Charlie Chipchase would also be in the library reading lots of books, but he would never say hello or talk to them.)

The library had books for everyone, and George Bum always liked the comic book section.

Brian Brackbrick and George Bum's favourite comic book superhero was called Captain Awesome.

The library had shelves and shelves full of Captain Awesome's adventures fighting against his legion of enemies, such as the Glue-Man, Baron Goldpants, Major Mayhem, Captain Chaos, and Dr. I. Diddit.

Anything they needed to know – if Brian Brackbrick did not already know it – they would find it in the library.

Brian Brackbrick and George Bum had stopped the Yoghurt Inferno last summer using information from:

- a science book called Properties of Liquid Under Pressure;
- a cookery book called 1001 Yummy Yoghurt Recipes;
- and, a very old Victorian story called I Say, What a Frightful Mess!

The first thing you saw as you went into the library was the desk of Dr. Harley Letters, the librarian. It was a big, oak desk, piled high with books and papers.

On the desk was a nameplate, which said:

Dr. Harley Letters, Librarian – Doctor of Books and Reading, not a Hospital Doctor, so I can't help you if you fall over or bang your arm or something like that (it was a very long nameplate).

Dr. Harley Letters always dressed smartly, and seemed to be very old indeed, but he was full of energy, and he always knew exactly where to find every single book.

As Brian Brackbrick and George Bum walked into the library today, though, Dr. Harley Letters was sitting very still behind his desk. He did not move or speak, and he seemed to be staring into space. On his head he was wearing a purple beret which Brian Brackbrick and George Bum had not seen before.

"Dr. Letters?" said Brian Brackbrick. Dr. Letters did not respond.

“DR. LETTERS!” shouted George Bum, but still nothing.

“I am going to snap Dr. Letters out of it, George,” said Brian Brackbrick.

“Okay, Brian,” said George Bum. “Shall I fetch a book on how to hypnotise people?”

“No need, George,” said Brian Brackbrick.

“A book on first aid?” suggested George Bum.

“No thank you, George,” said Brian Brackbrick.

“A book on the world’s strangest medical mysteries?” asked George Bum.

"I will not need that, thank you, George," said Brian Brackbrick.

"A comic book where Captain Awesome is trapped by the Glue-Man and has to be rescued?" George Bum really did try to be the most helpful friend.

"Watch this, George," said Brian Brackbrick, and he picked up a book from the desk. "DR. LETTERS!" Brian Brackbrick shouted. "I AM GOING TO STEAL THIS BOOK FROM THE LIBRARY!"

"Brian!" said George Bum, shocked. Then he looked at Dr. Letters, and he saw that his face was starting to twitch, and his mouth was starting to move.

Brian Brackbrick carried on: "I AM GOING TO STEAL **ALL** THE BOOKS FROM THIS LIBRARY!"

Suddenly, in one movement, Dr. Harley Letters took the beret from his head, stood up, and held one wagging finger up in the air. "You mustn't!" said Dr. Letters. "Stealing is wrong, it says so in at least six-hundred and twenty-eight books that I can think of!"

Dr. Harley Letters looked around in surprise, and he seemed to notice Brian Brackbrick and George Bum for the first time. "Oh, hello boys.

What's going on here? Did someone say something about stealing?"

"Certainly not, Dr. Letters," said Brian Brackbrick. "You must have been daydreaming." George Bum looked relieved. Dr. Letters sat down again.

"I see you have a new beret, Dr. Letters," said Brian Brackbrick. "Where did you get it from?"

"That young fellow from the hat shop brought it in this morning," said Dr. Letters. "The new chap, what's his name, Harry Hatman, yes, that's it. Strangest thing."

"What was strange about it, Dr. Letters?" asked George Bum.

"Well, the chap came into the library to introduce himself, wearing the most enormous hat I've ever seen," said Dr. Letters. "He could barely fit though the door. He said he'd brought me this beret as a gift. He was so insistent that I tried it on, right then and there. So I did, and the next thing I know, you two chaps are standing there. Very strange."

"Very strange indeed, Dr. Letters," said Brian Brackbrick.

"Do you know what happened to Old Mr. Hatston?" asked George Bum.

"Well, I did ask him that, this new fellow. He said he had no idea, that he had never heard of him." Dr. Letters sighed. "I suppose Mr. Hatston is living peacefully in the countryside, or on an adventure around the world, or somewhere in between."

"Do you know who Mr. Sparker is, Dr. Letters?" asked Brian Brackbrick.

"Yes, of course," said Dr. Letters. "All the shops along the main street, the buildings belong to Mr. Sparker. A lot of the houses, too. He must be very wealthy. Just a moment," he said, walking over to a shelf marked Local History.

Dr. Letters picked up a book and began to flip through the pages. "I believe that Mr. Sparker has been around for a long time, since before I moved here. Ah, here we are," he said, holding the book open so that Brian Brackbrick and George Bum could both see.

In the book was an old black-and-white photograph of a line of people. Some of the people looked familiar to Brian Brackbrick and George Bum.

“Here are all the people who worked in the shops in the old days,” said Dr. Letters. “There’s Mr. Hatston, when he was young Mr. Hatston. There’s Mrs. Blumenhole from the flower shop, when she was young Miss Petal. There’s

Constable Coving, he's retired now, of course. There's Mrs. Sprinkle, Fancy Nancy's mother. Well, look at that, how strange."

Dr. Letters pointed to a figure in the middle of the photograph – or rather, where a figure should have been. Someone had been cut out of the photograph…

"This is dreadful!" said Dr. Letters. "Someone has vandalised this book! Who would do such a thing?"

"Who has been cut out of the photograph, Dr. Letters?" asked Brian Brackbrick.

"Why, Mr. Sparker, of course! This is the only known photograph of him!" Dr. Letters slumped back into his chair, sadly.

"We're sorry about your book, Dr. Letters," said George Bum.

"Thank you, boys, and I am sorry that I can't give you the answers you are looking for," said Dr. Letters. "It seems this is the first time I have been unable to help you."

"Thank you for trying, Dr. Letters," said Brian Brackbrick, and with that, they left the library and headed for home.

CHAPTER 7:

MR. BRACKBRICK AND THE BOWLER HAT

When Brian Brackbrick and George Bum got home, Mr. Brackbrick was very eager to see Brian Brackbrick's new hat.

"I'm very eager to see your new hat, Brian," said Mr. Brackbrick. "What did you think of the new hat shop? What is Harry Hatman like?"

"This has been a rather strange morning," said Brian Brackbrick, as he handed over the hatbox to Mr. Brackbrick. "I asked Mr. Hatman for a new light-coloured Panama hat, but he gave me a new bowler hat instead."

"But you already have a bowler hat, a very smart one!" said Mr. Brackbrick.

"That is exactly what I tried to tell Mr. Hatman!" said Brian Brackbrick.

"He wouldn't listen, Mr. Brackbrick," said George Bum. "He's nothing like Old Mr. Hatston."

"Brian…" Mr. Brackbrick said as he opened the hatbox. "Did you try this bowler hat on in the hat shop?"

"Of course not!" Brian Brackbrick said. "Today is not a bowler hat day!"

"Well, this bowler hat looks too big for you, Brian," said Mr. Brackbrick. "It's almost too big even for me."

Mr. Brackbrick took the bowler hat out of the hatbox. Brian Brackbrick and George Bum could see that he was right, it was far too big. It was definitely a hat for a grown-up. Mr. Brackbrick put the hat on his head, and it was indeed almost too big even for him.

"I do not think Harry Hatman is the right person to be working in the hat shop," said Brian Brackbrick. "I wonder if he really knows anything about hats at all. I wish Old Mr. Hatston was still there. Harry Hatman said he had never heard of him."

"Um, Brian…" George Bum tried to interrupt.

"Yes, I will get to that part, George," said Brian Brackbrick. "Then we went into Nancy's cake shop, and she didn't know what had happened to Old Mr. Hatston."

"Brian, look!" George Bum tried again to interrupt.

"Yes, I am getting there, George," said Brian Brackbrick. "Then we went to the library, and Dr. Letters was acting strange at first, he looked like – "

"Like that, Brian!" said George Bum, pointing at Mr. Brackbrick.

Since the moment he had put on the bowler hat, Mr. Brackbrick had been standing still, staring into space, and he didn't seem to have heard anything that Brian Brackbrick had said to him.

"Yes, like that, George!" said Brian Brackbrick. "Quickly, remove the hat!"

George Bum jumped up and grabbed the hat from Mr. Brackbrick's head. Mr. Brackbrick blinked a few times, and then carried on as if nothing had happened.

"Yes, it's definitely too big for you, Brian," said Mr. Brackbrick, taking the bowler hat from George Bum and putting it back into the hatbox. "You should take the hat back to the hat shop." He paused. "Or perhaps I should go to the hat shop, I must go to the hat shop…"

Mr. Brackbrick blinked again and shook his head. "What was I saying? Oh, yes, take the bowler hat back to the hat shop. I have made some sandwiches for you both, they are in the kitchen. I am going to have an afternoon nap, I suddenly feel rather tired." Mr. Brackbrick sat down in his comfy armchair.

Brian Brackbrick and George Bum went into the kitchen to eat their sandwiches. "Shall we go back to the hat shop, Brian?" asked George Bum. "Well, we could do that, George," said Brian Brackbrick. "Or…"

"Or what, Brian?" said George Bum.

"George, I have an idea," said Brian Brackbrick. "I would like to try an experiment!"

CHAPTER 8:

BRIAN BRACKBRICK TRIES AN EXPERIMENT

After they had finished their sandwiches, Brian Brackbrick and George Bum went to check on Mr. Brackbrick, who was in his comfy armchair, sound asleep.

“Please pass me the over-sized bowler hat, George,” whispered Brian Brackbrick, as he tiptoed over to Mr. Brackbrick.

“What do you want it for, Brian?” asked George Bum as he handed it over.

“I am going to carefully place the bowler hat on his head,” said Brian Brackbrick.

“Why, Brian?” asked George Bum. “We should take the bowler hat back to the hat shop.”

“Do not worry, George, I expect we will end up in the hat shop soon enough!” Brian Brackbrick placed the bowler hat on Mr. Brackbrick’s head.

Suddenly Mr. Brackbrick’s eyes opened and he sat bolt upright.

"Mr. Brackbrick? Are you okay?" asked George Bum. Mr. Brackbrick did not respond. "What should we do now, Brian?"

"This is an experiment, George!" said Brian Brackbrick. "We must see what happens!"

So they waited, to see what would happen.

Nothing happened.

They waited for a bit longer.

Still nothing happened.

"Nothing is happening, Brian," said George Bum, and he leaned closer to Mr. Brackbrick's face. "Can you talk to us, Mr. Brackbrick?"

"I CAN TALK TO YOU!" shouted Mr. Brackbrick, making George Bum jump. Mr. Brackbrick's eyes still seemed to be looking into the distance.

"Well done, George," said Brian Brackbrick. "I wonder…"

Brian Brackbrick also leaned closer to Mr. Brackbrick's face. "You would like to buy me the biggest hat ever made in the history of the world ever."

Mr. Brackbrick repeated, loudly, "I WOULD LIKE TO BUY YOU THE BIGGEST HAT EVER MADE IN THE HISTORY OF THE WORLD EVER!"

"This is incredible!" said Brian Brackbrick. "You would like to buy me a thousand hats! Two thousand hats!"

Mr. Brackbrick said, loudly, "I WOULD LIKE TO BUY YOU THREE THOUSAND HATS!"

"Um, Brian?" said George Bum. "I don't think we should take advantage."

Brian Brackbrick had been almost dizzy with excitement, but the wise words of George Bum calmed him down. "Yes, you are right, George. I think our experiment is a success, and it is now time to return to the hat shop!"

Mr. Brackbrick shouted, "HAT SHOP!" and stood up quickly. "I MUST GO TO THE HAT SHOP! I MUST GO AT ONCE!"

Mr. Brackbrick turned on his heels and walked straight out of the front door, and off he went down the street, without even stopping to put his shoes on.

Brian Brackbrick and George Bum looked at each other, shocked, and then they both ran after Mr. Brackbrick.

Mr. Brackbrick had reached the corner of the main street by the time Brian Brackbrick and George Bum caught up with him; he was walking in a very funny way, like he was a puppet being controlled by invisible strings.

Mr. Brackbrick seemed to know where he was going, but he took no notice of what was around him. Brian Brackbrick and George Bum had to keep him safe by steering him away from danger.

“Do not cross the road yet!” said Brian Brackbrick, as they waited for a car to drive past.

"I WILL NOT CROSS THE ROAD YET!" shouted Mr. Brackbrick as he stopped his funny walk.

"You can cross the road now!" said George Bum, once the road was clear.

"I WILL CROSS THE ROAD NOW!" shouted Mr. Brackbrick, and off he went again.

"Do not step in that big pile of dog poo!" warned Brian Brackbrick.

"I WILL NOT STEP IN THAT BIG PILE OF DOG POO!" shouted Mr. Brackbrick.

By now the three of them were creating quite a scene, and quite a few people were wondering what was going on. Brian Brackbrick and George Bum were concentrating so much on keeping Mr. Brackbrick safe that they didn't notice all the people in and around the shops watching them.

Mr. Brackbrick would not speak to anyone they walked past, so Brian Brackbrick and George Bum had to help him with that too, as they did not want anyone to think that he was rude.

Frankie Featherface, who ran the pet shop, walked towards them. Brian Brackbrick whispered, “You should say ‘good afternoon’ to Mr. Featherface.”

So Mr. Brackbrick shouted, “I SHOULD SAY ‘GOOD AFTERNOON’ TO MR. FEATHERFACE!”

“Well, good afternoon, Mr. Brackbrick,” said Frankie Featherface, looking puzzled as he walked on.

When they walked past Morris Hawkwind, who ran the music shop, Brian Brackbrick whispered, “You should say ‘good afternoon’ quietly to Mr. Hawkwind.”

Mr. Brackbrick seemed to shout even louder, “I SHOULD SAY ‘GOOD AFTERNOON’ **QUIETLY** TO MR. HAWKWIND!”

Morris Hawkwind looked thoroughly confused, but he said, “Good afternoon to you, dudes,” as he walked along the street clicking his fingers.

Soon they saw Charlie Chipchase approaching, and they could not resist this opportunity. Brian

Brackbrick whispered, “Say ‘Charlie Chipchase smells like mud.’”

Mr. Brackbrick shouted, “CHARLIE CHIPCHASE SMELLS LIKE MUD!”

Charlie Chipchase was shocked to hear this, and he started to cross the road to avoid them.

George Bum whispered, “Say ‘Charlie Chipchase always wears his grandad’s old pants.’”

So Mr. Brackbrick shouted, “CHARLIE CHIPCHASE ALWAYS WEARS HIS GRANDAD’S OLD PANTS!”

Charlie Chipchase looked over his shoulder at them and shouted, “No I don’t! I have brand new pants every day, they’re really expensive!”

Brian Brackbrick and George Bum laughed until they realised that they had reached the hat shop. Without stopping, Mr. Brackbrick pushed open the door and went inside. Brian Brackbrick and George Bum followed him in.

CHAPTER 9:

MR. BRACKBRICK FIGHTS THE POWER OF THE HAT

Brian Brackbrick and George Bum walked into the hat shop, and the door closed behind them. As Mr. Brackbrick walked up to the counter, Harry Hatman burst out from the back of the shop.

"H e e e e e e e e e e y y y y y y y y y you're back already! Wait a minute, who are you?" Harry Hatman said to Mr. Brackbrick.

"I AM MR. BRACKBRICK!" shouted Mr. Brackbrick.

"I see," said Harry Hatman. "That bowler hat was meant for young Brian Brackbrick, but never mind! You have brought him with you."

Harry Hatman quickly snatched the baseball cap from Brian Brackbrick's head and placed it on the counter. Brian Brackbrick was shocked.

"I AM IN THE HAT SHOP!" shouted Mr. Brackbrick, which made Harry Hatman jump. The enormous Stetson hat wobbled on his head.

"Yes, yes, very good," said Harry Hatman.

"What's going on, Mr. Hatman?" asked George Bum.

"Why did you want me to wear that bowler hat, Mr. Hatman?" asked Brian Brackbrick.

"Well, boys," said Harry Hatman. "I was told that – "

"I AM IN THE HAT SHOP!" shouted Mr. Brackbrick again, which made Harry Hatman jump even more, and he had to stop the enormous Stetson hat from falling off his head.

"Stop that!" Harry Hatman said to Mr. Brackbrick.

"I WILL STOP SAYING, 'I AM IN THE HAT SHOP!'" shouted Mr. Brackbrick.

Harry Hatman sighed. “These hats need a lot of work. Anyway, what was I saying? Oh yes. I was told that whenever something happens in this town, it’s always you, Brian Brackbrick, and you, George Bum, who interfere and stop it! Always getting in the way – but not any longer!”

Harry Hatman reached behind the counter and brought up a woolly hat. “The days of Brian Brackbrick and George Bum interfering in Mr. Sparker’s plans are over!” Harry Hatman said, and he gave the woolly hat to Mr. Brackbrick.

“Take this hat, Mr. Brackbrick,” said Harry Hatman.

"I AM MR. BRACKBRICK!" shouted Mr. Brackbrick. "I AM TAKING THE HAT FROM YOU, STRANGELY-DRESSED MAN!"

"Put the hat," said Harry Hatman, smiling, "on the head of Brian Brackbrick."

"Run, Brian!" shouted George Bum.

Brian Brackbrick tried to run, but with the shop counter on one side, and Harry Hatman on the other, he had nowhere to go. Brian Brackbrick slowly backed away, until he touched the thick shelves and could go no further.

Mr. Brackbrick walked towards him slowly, holding out the woolly hat. “I WILL PUT THE HAT ON – ON – ”

“No! Stop!” said Brian Brackbrick. Mr. Brackbrick stopped, and stood frozen in place.

“Put the hat on his head!” shouted Harry Hatman. “Go on, do it!”

Mr. Brackbrick tried to fight it. "I WILL PUT THE HAT ON – NO I WILL NOT – "

Just as it seemed that Mr. Brackbrick could not fight it any longer, the door to the hat shop flew open. In burst Sergeant Shelley Shiplap, with some of the people from the town. People had noticed Mr. Brackbrick's strange behaviour on the way to the shop, and they had called Sergeant Shiplap.

With her was Dr. Harley Letters, Fancy Nancy (carrying a tray of cupcakes, of course), Frankie Featherface, Morris Hawkwind, and Raymond Rings, who ran the jewellery shop.

"Evening all!" said Sergeant Shiplap (even though it was still the afternoon). "What is going on here, Mr. Hatman?"

"You're too late!" said Harry Hatman. "Soon Brian Brackbrick will be under my control, and then nothing will stop Mr. Sparker!"

Everyone turned to look at Mr. Brackbrick and Brian Brackbrick. Mr. Brackbrick was fighting it, but the woolly hat was almost on Brian Brackbrick's head…

Seeing that there was no time to lose, George Bum quickly snatched a cupcake from Nancy's tray, took aim, and threw the cupcake as hard as he could.

Everyone watched the cupcake as it flew through the air, and hit the bowler hat on Mr. Brackbrick's head. (George Bum had a very good aim.)

The bowler hat slid from Mr. Brackbrick's head and fell to the floor. Mr. Brackbrick blinked a few times and shook his head. "What am I doing here?" he said. "Where are my shoes? Why aren't I wearing any shoes?"

Brian Brackbrick picked up the bowler hat, and handed it to Sergeant Shelley Shiplap. "Sergeant Shiplap, please look inside this bowler hat. You will see that it is full of wires, flashing lights and twiddly bits. So is that woolly hat, and probably all the hats in this shop."

Sergeant Shiplap looked inside the bowler hat, and saw that it was indeed full of wires, flashing lights and twiddly bits.

"Goodness me," said Sergeant Shiplap. "Mr. Harry Hatman, you are under arrest! Come with me at once! I will return later to confiscate all these hats, for evidence! Evening all!"

Sergeant Shiplap led Harry Hatman out of the shop. As everyone stood aside to let them pass, Harry Hatman shouted, "Mr. Sparker will not be happy about this!"

Everyone congratulated Brian Brackbrick and George Bum. Dr. Letters gave Brian Brackbrick's baseball cap back to him, then told a very confused Mr. Brackbrick what had happened. Mr. Brackbrick was still tightly gripping the woolly hat.

Brian Brackbrick said quietly to George Bum, "I only wanted a new hat!"

CHAPTER 10: BRIAN BRACKBRICK AND GEORGE BUM RECEIVE ANOTHER MEDAL

Later that day, everyone from the town gathered at the front of the library to watch as Brian Brackbrick and George Bum were presented with a medal each by Lord Mayor Spencer. Brian Brackbrick was wearing a very smart black trilby hat.

(Mr. Brackbrick had, without realising it, taken home the woolly hat from Harry Hatman's shop. Brian Brackbrick had put it away in a hatbox at the back of a shelf where it would be safe.)

Everyone cheered as Lord Mayor Spencer introduced Brian Brackbrick and George Bum.

Everyone seemed happy, except Mrs. Blumenhole from the flower shop, who looked as if she was quite sad.

"It gives me great pleasure," said Lord Mayor Spencer, "great pleasure indeed, oh yes, to award these medals to young Brian Brackbrick and young George Bum. Ho ho, you two just can't stop yourselves from going around and getting into things, can you? You two certainly are busybodies, oh I mean to say, you are busy boys. Ho ho."

"Last summer," Lord Mayor Spencer went on, "you two young heroes saved the cake shop from a terrible Yoghurt Inferno, and now you have saved my wonderful town from the hazard of Harry Hatman. We can certainly rely on you when things go wrong. Ho ho. Let us have more cheers and applause for Brian Brackbrick and George Bum!"

Brian Brackbrick and George Bum were very pleased to get another medal. George Bum could see, though, that Brian Brackbrick was doing a lot of thinking.

Brian Brackbrick was thinking:

What happened to Old Mr. Hatston?

What did Mrs. Blumenhole know?

Who was Mr. Sparker…?

FIND OUT

NEXT TIME!

BRIAN BRACKBRICK

AND GEORGE BUM

WILL RETURN!

IN...

BRIAN BRACKBRICK AND THE MYSTERY OF MRS. BLUMENHOLE

COMING SOON!

A WORD FROM BRIAN BRACKBRICK

Thank you for reading all about my adventures!

Look out for the next story – join George Bum and I as we search for Old Mr. Hatston, and see what Mrs. Blumenhole has been doing!

A WORD FROM BRIAN BRACKBRICK

Maybe we will find out who Mr. Sparker is too. I certainly hope so...

In the meantime, you can send me a message to say hello!

brianbrackbrick@googlemail.com

A WORD FROM BRIAN BRACKBRICK

Everyone who sends me a message will receive a special sneak preview of the next book!

See you next time!

Brian Brackbrick

Printed in Great Britain
by Amazon